MONGOL WARRIORS

by Lois Sepahban

Published by The Child's World®
1980 Lookout Drive • Mankato, MN 56003-1705
800-599-READ • www.childsworld.com

ACKNOWLEDGMENTS
The Child's World®: Mary Berendes, Publishing Director
Red Line Editorial: Editorial direction
The Design Lab: Design
Amnet: Production
Content Consultant: Timothy May, PhD, Professor of Central
Eurasian History, University of North Georgia
Design elements: iStockphoto
Photographs ©: Stapleton Collection/Corbis, cover, 4,
30 (bottom left); North Wind Picture Archives, 9, 22;
Steven Wright/Shutterstock Images, 10; Public Domain,
12, 25; Bettmann/Corbis, 13; Ng Han Guan/AP Images, 17;
Nick Hewetson/Thinkstock, 18; Burstein Collection/Corbis,
21, 30 (top); Keren Su/Corbis, 26, 30 (bottom right)

ISBN 9781631437564
LCCN 2014945429

Printed in the United States of America
Mankato, MN
November, 2014
PA02246

ABOUT THE AUTHOR

Lois Sepahban has written several books for children, covering science, history, biography, and fiction topics. She lives in Kentucky with her husband and two children.

TABLE OF CONTENTS

Temujin later became known as Genghis Khan.

CHAPTER ONE

TEMUJIN'S PROMISE

In the summer of 1203, Temujin was prepared to fight. He was the Mongol chief of the Borjigin tribe. His enemy was his former teacher Toghril. Toghril was the chief of the Kereit tribe. The Mongols were **nomads** who lived in central Asia. As nomads, the Mongols did not build towns or cities. Instead they traveled with their animals to different pastures.

Temujin gathered 19 loyal men and set up a camp close to Toghril's army. His warriors were exhausted and injured after many battles. They could have deserted Temujin, but they did not. These Mongol warriors were loyal to Temujin. They were willing to die for him.

Temujin had a plan. He sent spies to his enemy's camp. When the moment was right, he attacked the enemy's camp by surprise. After three days of fighting, Temujin and his warriors won.

Temujin slowly rose to power after surviving a tough childhood. Other chiefs were afraid of young Temujin. They feared that the Mongols might become loyal to Temujin. The worried chiefs tried to hurt Temujin in many ways. The Taychiut tribe kidnapped him. His family's horses were stolen. Temujin faced each challenge with bravery. His bravery made others want to follow him.

At that time, one chief ruled each tribe. It had been many years since a leader ruled over all the Mongol tribes. But in times of trouble, the Mongol tribes united. In 1206, the tribes united and chose Temujin as their leader. They gave him a new name: Genghis Khan. From that day forward, he ruled all the Mongol tribes. Genghis Khan was the Mongol leader for 20 years. He used military strength to rule his great empire.

TOUGH CHILDHOOD

Temujin's tough childhood prepared him to become a powerful warrior. When Temujin was nine years old, men from the Tatar tribe killed his father. Temujin's father, Yesugei, was the grandson of Khabul Khan. Khabul Khan was the last great leader to rule over all of the Mongol tribes. After his father's murder, their tribe abandoned Temujin's small family. The family survived by eating roots, berries, mice, and fish. Temujin and his brothers practiced their warrior skills. They learned **archery**. They grew strong.

ANOTHER VIEW
NEED FOR PASTURES

Mongol leaders needed to control large areas of land. Tribes needed enough pasture for their herds and horses. When they went to war, Mongol armies needed to plan where they would find pasture for their animals. How do you think the need for pastures affected the Mongols' decisions to invade other countries?

CHAPTER TWO

RISE OF THE MONGOLS

Even before Genghis Khan's rise to power, constant battle was a way of life for the Mongol tribes. They fought to gain control of land. The tribes kept large herds of sheep, goats, cows, and horses. The tribe that controlled the most pasture had the strongest herds.

Every Mongol tribe wanted to protect its land. Even if tribes were not at war, warriors were prepared to fight. Entire tribes, including women, children, and **elders**, helped warriors prepare for war. They kept weapons in good condition. They made food for the warriors. Everyone was ready to pack up at any moment to follow the chief's command.

Mongol tribes needed land for their herds.

In 1206, war became more of a focus in Mongol society. But instead of fighting each other, the united Mongol tribes focused on the south. The Tangut Empire and the Jin Empire were both part of present-day China. In Genghis Khan's time, these empires were known for their riches. The Jin feared that if the Mongol tribes were united, the Mongols would become more powerful than them. The Mongols wanted the riches of the Tangut and Jin empires. They also wanted the Jin to leave them alone.

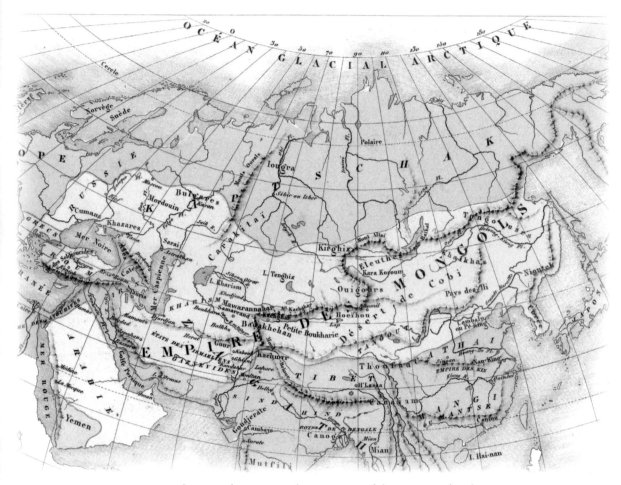

Around 1243, the Mongol Empire (in blue) stretched
across Asia and the Middle East.

Genghis Khan's first step as ruler was to organize the
tribes. He had an army of thousands of warriors. By 1207,
the Mongol armies were organized into fighting units and
trained to work together. By 1215, the Mongol army had
conquered the Tangut and the Jin. The Mongols took

every item of value. They destroyed palaces and other important buildings. They killed anyone who stood in their way.

Genghis Khan, his sons, and his grandsons led the Mongol army for the next 20 years. They expanded the Mongol Empire into eastern parts of Europe, the Middle East, and most of Asia. In 1223, the Mongol Empire was vast. It stretched from the Pacific Ocean on the coast of modern-day China to the Caspian Sea in western Asia.

In 1227, Genghis Khan became sick and died. He was about 60 years old. After Genghis Khan's death, his son Ogedei became the Mongol leader. Before Ogedei died in 1241, the Mongols defeated Russia and Poland. The next strong leader was chosen in 1251. He was Mongke, Genghis Khan's grandson. During Mongke's reign, the Mongols destroyed Baghdad. This is the capital of present-day Iraq. They killed thousands of people there, including the ruler. Mongke died in 1259.

The leaders who followed Mongke could not keep the Mongol Empire together. Some of

Mongke (with crown) ruled the Mongol Empire for eight years.

Kublai Khan's fleet of ships sailed to parts of Asia.

Genghis Khan's sons and grandsons became rulers of the lands the Mongols had conquered. In 1264, Mongke's brother Kublai Khan became the leader of Mongolian lands. Kublai Khan went on to conquer all of China in 1279. He became the first emperor of the Chinese Yuan **dynasty**, ruling over nearly all eastern parts of Asia.

Fierce and Fair

Genghis Khan was known as a fierce warrior and brave leader. He was also known for being fair to those who were loyal. This was unusual for a Mongol chief. But Genghis Khan was ruthless, too. It was the combination of all of these qualities that made the Mongol people so loyal to Genghis Khan.

Another View
MONGOL WOMEN

Mongol women raised children, cared for animals, cooked, and made dairy products, such as yogurt and cheese. They were expert horse riders as well. Women also practiced archery and some fought in battle. But men had the most power in their society. What do you think it was like to be a Mongol woman in ancient times?

CHAPTER THREE

ARMOR AND WEAPONS

In Genghis Khan's time, all Mongol boys were raised to be warriors. The warrior's most important weapon was the bow and arrow. Warriors carried two or three bows into battle with them. A Mongol warrior made his war bow. This process could take up to one year to finish.

Warriors also carried up to 60 arrows. Mongol arrows were designed for different purposes. Some arrows were for close targets. Other arrows traveled longer distances. Warriors could shoot arrows almost 900 feet (270 m). Some could pierce armor. Some had tips that could be lit on fire. And some whistled to scare enemies.

Mongol boys began using bows and arrows when they were four or five years old. A boy was ready for his first battle at 16 or 17 years old. By then, the warrior had more than ten years of daily practice with the bow and arrow. He had a strong upper body to use his powerful war bow.

The Mongol army was a **cavalry**. Cavalry are warriors who ride horses. All were trained to fight on horseback. Mongol warriors could shoot their arrows while riding at full gallop on their horses. That made the warriors quick and deadly.

Warriors carried a lasso, saber, dagger, shield, and saddlebag into battle. The shield was made of wood strips and covered with leather. Many warriors also carried two or three **javelins** and a lance with a hook on the end. This lance could pull enemies off their horses. A saber was a light, sharp sword used in close combat.

A warrior's saddlebag held food, a change of clothes, and tools. The saddlebag could also be inflated to float in water. This was helpful when a Mongol army crossed a river. Mongol warriors often wore helmets,

Modern Mongol soldiers wear traditional warrior costumes during a ceremony in 2006.

Warriors used different weapons in battle.

long coats, and leather boots. They also wore chain
mail and leather plates to protect their bodies. A silk
shirt underneath helped keep arrows from deeply
piercing warriors' bodies.

Warriors and Horses

A warrior's horses were his most prized possessions. Mongol children were taught to ride horses at three years old. In battle, warriors brought at least five or six horses. This made it possible to ride for many miles a day. They changed horses as the animals grew tired. If warriors ran out of food, they could drink their horses' blood or eat their meat. Horses were important for spiritual reasons, too. The fastest or strongest horses were sometimes worshipped. And powerful chieftains were buried with a mare, a stallion, and a foal.

AnotherView
Mongol Childhood

Childhood was harsh for Mongol children. It was common for women or children to be kidnapped by enemy tribes. Kidnapped children often became slaves. Childhood was also a time of training, rather than play. Boys and girls learned to ride horses. They also trained with bows and arrows and knives. Families moved from place to place with their herds. How was Mongol childhood similar to or different from yours?

CHAPTER FOUR

BATTLE TACTICS

Mongol warriors were known for being ruthless, fast, and organized. When the Mongol army was on the move, the group could stretch for miles. Warriors communicated with each other by using flags, smoke, and drums. Other armies in the 1200s moved slowly. Unlike the Mongols, they had many foot soldiers and supply wagons.

Genghis Khan organized his army in groups of ten, 100, 1,000, and 10,000 warriors. There were 95 commanders in charge of a group of 1,000 warriors. Genghis Khan's generals were skilled enough to take command if another general was killed. And his warriors were so well trained that they followed their leader's commands without question. Mongol generals could quickly move a small or large group of warriors on a single command.

In open battle, the Mongol army divided into three groups. One part of their army pretended to retreat. At the same time, a second part of their army waited in position to attack enemies as they chased the retreating warriors. The third group was ready to surround enemies as they chased the

Some warriors hid while other warriors fought.

Genghis Khan led the Mongol warriors into battle.

Mongol warriors. By the time the enemy army knew what was happening, it was too late to escape.

Some Mongol battles took place in cities and towns. First the Mongol army laid **siege** to the town. They surrounded the town. The Mongol army could not get in and the townspeople could not get out. It gave the town some time for **allies** to arrive and help. But it could be dangerous, too. If a siege lasted long enough, the people inside the town ran out of food and possibly water. The Mongol army used catapults, gunpowder, and crossbows to break down town walls. They could then enter the city and take control.

The Secret History of the Mongols

Not long after the death of Genghis Khan, an unknown **scribe** wrote *The Secret History of the Mongols*. It tells the story of how the Mongol people came to be. It also describes Genghis Khan's birth, life, and death. *The Secret History of the Mongols* is the only record written about Genghis Khan in the Mongolian language. The author also lived during Genghis Khan's lifetime. Until the end of the Mongol Empire, only members of the Mongol royalty were allowed to read this book.

Another View

The Conquered

There was almost no chance of escape for people captured in battle by Mongol warriors. Most prisoners became slaves or were used as human shields. The captured men were forced to march in front of Mongol warriors. And when Mongol warriors captured enemy troops running away from battle, the Mongols killed them because they were disloyal to their leader. Mongol warriors forced some female prisoners to become their wives. How do you think a prisoner felt about being captured by the Mongol army?

CHAPTER FIVE

MAJOR MONGOL BATTLES

The fighting between Mongol tribes was fierce.
It included kidnapping, poisoning, and murder.
When the Mongol army marched west, it earned its
reputation for being very brutal.

In 1216, the Mongols had defeated the Tangut
and Jin. The battling could have stopped. But Genghis
Khan's men were warriors. Genghis Khan's army grew
as his territory grew. His warriors wanted riches.
They wanted to make war.

Khwarazm was a state near lands controlled
by the Mongols. In 1218, Genghis Khan sent an
ambassador to the ruler of Khwarazm. Genghis
Khan wanted Khwarazm to trade with the Mongols.

The ruler of Khwarazm flees across a river to escape the Mongol army.

Kublai Khan led the Mongol army to Ta-li and into battle.

The ruler of Khwarazm killed Genghis Khan's ambassador. Genghis Khan was outraged.

Every Mongol man between age 17 and 60 rode in Genghis Khan's army. As revenge for the death of their ambassador, Mongol warriors killed thousands of people. The governor of Khwarazm was brutally killed. After the defeat of the town of Nishapur in Khwarazm, all men, women, and children were killed. The ruler of Khwarazm died of a chest illness before the Mongol army could capture him.

Another famous battle involved Kublai Khan. In 1251, his older brother Mongke became the leader of the Mongols. While Mongke was away at battle, Kublai Khan was in charge of the Mongol lands in northern China. In 1252, Mongke told Kublai Khan to conquer the kingdom of Ta-li.

During the summer of 1253, Kublai Khan and his army set out for Ta-li. To get there, they had to cross mountains and rivers. When the Mongol army arrived in Ta-li that fall, Kublai Khan sent three ambassadors to the king of Ta-li. The ambassadors were to tell the king to submit to the Mongol army or there would be war. The king's minister had the ambassadors killed.

This angered the Mongols. In October 1253, Kublai Khan divided his army into three groups. One group attacked from the west, one group attacked from the east, and Kublai Khan led a group on a direct attack.

The Ta-li army gathered by the Yangtze River. Kublai Khan's soldiers made rafts and crossed the river during the night. The Ta-li army did not expect the night attack. Many Ta-li soldiers were killed. The rest retreated to the city of Ta-li.

Kublai Khan sent a message to the people of Ta-li. If they surrendered peacefully, he would not kill them. The people surrendered. When the Mongols captured the king's minister, they beheaded him. And when the men who helped kill the Mongol ambassadors were captured, they were also killed. But everyone else in Ta-li was safe. Kublai Khan kept his word. He did not kill the king of Ta-li or the family of the king's minister.

At its peak, the Mongol Empire covered more than 11 million square miles (28 million sq km), including nearly all of Asia and eastern parts of Europe. Genghis Khan and later Mongol leaders set up trade routes that were used by European travelers, such as Marco Polo. These leaders united the tribes to form an empire. Mongol warriors were a powerful force in the ancient world.

ANOTHER VIEW
THE *YAM*

As Genghis Khan conquered lands, he needed to be able to send messages from one part of his empire to the other. The *yam* was a system of roads that could be used by those with a special passport called a *paiza*. The roads had post stations and places for traders to stop for supplies. How do you think this system helped Genghis Khan rule the Mongol Empire?

KUBLAI KHAN

After the death of Mongke, Kublai Khan became the leader of the Mongols in 1260. He also became the emperor of China. He founded the Yuan dynasty, which lasted for approximately 100 years. Kublai Khan became more like a Chinese ruler and less like a Mongol ruler. He gave up being a nomad and wanted to live in a palace. As the Mongol leaders became less warlike, their empire became smaller.

TIMELINE

1206
Temujin becomes ruler of the Mongol tribes. He receives a new name: Genghis Khan.

1215
By this time, the Mongol army conquers the Tangut Empire and Jin Empire.

1223
The Mongol Empire stretches across Asia, the Middle East, and into Europe.

1227
Genghis Khan dies.

1227–1259
The sons and grandsons of Genghis Khan rule the Mongols after his death.

1264
Kublai Khan rules the Mongol Empire. He also becomes emperor of China.

GLOSSARY

allies (AL-lyes) Allies are people or groups who join together for a common purpose, such as to fight a war. A town under siege waited for its allies to help.

ambassador (am-BASS-uh-dur) An ambassador is a person sent by a government to represent it in a different country. The ruler of Khwarazm killed Genghis Khan's ambassador.

archery (AR-chuh-ree) Archery is the skill of shooting arrows at targets using bows and arrows. Mongol warriors learned archery at a young age.

cavalry (KAV-uhl-ree) Cavalry are soldiers who ride on horseback. All Mongol warriors were cavalry.

dynasty (DYE-nuh-stee) A dynasty is a series of rulers from the same family. Kublai Khan became the first emperor of the Yuan dynasty.

elders (EL-durz) Elders are older people. Even elders helped warriors prepare for battle.

javelins (JAV-uh-luhns) Javelins are light spears that can be thrown. Many warriors carried two or three javelins.

nomads (NOH-madz) Nomads are people who do not settle in one place, but instead roam from place to place. The Mongols were nomads.

scribe (SKRIBE) A scribe is a person who copies books or other documents by hand. An unknown scribe wrote *The Secret History of the Mongols*.

siege (SEEJ) A siege is when troops surround a city or other area to cause its people to surrender. The Mongol army laid siege to towns.

TO LEARN MORE

BOOKS

Bankston, John. *Genghis Khan*. Hockessin, DE: Mitchell Lane Publishers, 2014.

Bodden, Valerie. *Great Warriors: Mongols*. Mankato, MN: Creative Education, 2014.

Dittmar, Brian. *Mongol Warriors*. Minneapolis, MN: Bellwether Media, 2012.

WEB SITES

Visit our Web site for links about Mongol warriors:

childsworld.com/links

Note to Parents, Teachers, and Librarians: We routinely verify our Web links to make sure they are safe and active sites. So encourage your readers to check them out!

INDEX